D0476714
OUT OF THIS WORLD
000002040098

Published by Curious Fox, an imprint of Capstone Global Library Limited, 264
Banbury Road, Oxford, OX2 7DY – Registered company number: 6695582

www.curious-fox.com

Illustrations by Matthew Vimislik

All characters in this publication are fictitious and any resemblance to real persons, living or dead, is purely coincidental.

ISBN 978 1 782 02564 1
20 19 18 17 16
10 9 8 7 6 5 4 3 2 1

A CIP catalogue for this book is available from the British Library.

Printed and bound in China

OUT OF THIS WORLD

TROUBLE ON VENUS

by Raymond Bean

Curious Fox
a capstone company-publishers for children

CONTENTS

INTRODUCTION

My name is Starr. I'm just like every other ten-year-old girl I know, with one big difference: I live in space.

You see, my mum is a world-class astronaut, scientist and all-round super-genius. She was chosen to be the first person to move her entire family to space. Now she's not just my mum, she's also in charge of the world's most advanced space station.

Dad is a documentary filmmaker. He's making a movie about our family being the first family to ever live in space. It's not like we're actors or anything. He just films us doing our everyday stuff like eating, playing and brushing our teeth.

I have a thirteen-year-old brother called Apollo. He thinks he's cooler than winter.

Cosmo is my super-cute, five-year-old brother.

If you ask me, he *is* cooler than winter. We call him "Cozzie" for short.

We're helping to lead the new world of space tourism so that people can take holidays in space. I like to call them space holidays.

The head of the entire space programme is Mrs Sosa. She's my mum's boss. Her granddaughter, Tia, and I work together. Tia trains kids on Earth to get them ready for space. I help them with life in space once they're on the station.

My best friend, Allison, thinks I'll forget all about her now that I live in space, but just because I live in space doesn't mean I don't need my best friend.

I may be an ordinary girl, but my life is completely out of this world!

Chapter 1

LET'S DO THIS

"I can see Venus in the sky right now," Allison said. We were on a video call. Allison was at home in Colorado, USA, where I used to live. I was orbiting Venus in a spaceship.

"I can see it too," I said, taking in the view of the cloud-covered planet from my pod.

"From what I've read, the planet is a nasty place," Allison said.

"That's what everyone says, but so far all I've been able to see are really thick clouds covering it. It looks like a big, blurry snowball floating in space."

"What are you going to do there?" she asked.

"Mum says we'll do a lot of experiments to help learn more about Venus," I replied.

We always have a mix of scientists and tourists on the ship with us on our missions, and this mission was no different. The kids on my team were a girl named Yasmin and a boy named Lin. Yasmin was nine and Lin was twelve. They were picked specifically for the trip to Venus in a competition run by Mrs Sosa. Kids from all over the country sent in videos explaining why they should be given the opportunity to go to Venus. I didn't see the videos they sent in, but Mrs Sosa said Yasmin's and Lin's were the most impressive.

"Hi there," Allison said as Yasmin and Lin cruised into my room hanging on to the cruisers we use to move around the station.

Allison and I had talked so much on the way to Venus that Yasmin and Lin sort of knew her too. They waved, and then Lin said, "Starr, your mum is looking for you."

"She said we're almost ready to run our first experiment," Yasmin added.

"Allison, I'll talk to you later. We've got to go," I said, and then the three of us cruised off to find Mum. She was in the first place we looked: the control room. Cozzie sat on her lap, his hands on the controls.

"Hey, Starr!" Cozzie shouted. "Mum let me steer the ship. Can you believe that?"

Mum winked and nodded. "That's right. Your little brother just steered the most advanced spacecraft in the history of mankind."

"It was easy," Cozzie said sweetly.

Yasmin, Lin and I giggled.

"I hope you're all ready for our first experiment on Venus," Mum said.

"We're not going down there, are we?" I asked cautiously.

"Of course not!" Mum exclaimed.

I was relieved. Venus is the second planet from the Sun. The temperature is usually over 430 degrees Celsius! It's one of the most dangerous places in the entire solar system.

My brother Apollo cruised in. He was going way too fast . . . as usual.

"Apollo, how many times have I told you to slow down on your cruiser?" Mum asked.

My dad was right behind him and going just as fast on his cruiser. They had been racing.

"Sorry," Dad said.

Mum didn't look pleased. "You too?" she asked, looking even more frustrated.

"We were just having a little fun. Oh no . . . I forgot to bring my video equipment. I'll be right back," he added and zoomed out as quickly as he zoomed in.

Apollo apologized halfheartedly and took out his phone.

Usually, Apollo and I have our own separate teams of kids, but on this mission Mum put us on a team together with Yasmin and Lin. They were both really clever, but I was having a hard time managing them. We hadn't had any arguments or anything, but they were really competitive. They were always trying to outdo each other and me. It was kind of like having three Apollos around, because he always wants to be the best at everything.

Mum snapped me out of my daydream when she said, "Now that you're all here, do you kids want to know more about your first experiment on Venus?" Apollo put his phone away.

We all nodded as Dad cruised back, much slower this time, with his camera equipment. "Did you start yet?" he asked.

"I was just about to," Mum said.

"Perfect!" he exclaimed, holding up his camera. "Action!"

"You already know a little about Venus and the challenges it presents," Mum said. "And, as you know, humans have never actually visited Venus before."

"We've been sending unmanned spaceships to Venus since 1962, but we're the first humans to ever visit the planet," Yasmin added.

"Wasn't the first ship in 1967?" Lin asked.

"No, you're thinking of *Venera 4*. I'm talking about *Mariner 2*," Yasmin replied.

Yasmin and Lin had been bickering like this the entire trip. Mum and Dad didn't seem to see it, but I did. If I'm honest, I was getting tired of it.

"*Mariner 2* was the first to fly *by* Venus. *Venera 4* dropped to the surface and was never heard from again. So, it was technically the first ship to touch down on the surface," Lin said.

"*Venera 4* dropped a probe to the surface of Venus," Mum interrupted, "and that's exactly what you are going to do today. The probe from *Venera 4* measured temperature and pressure on Venus. It only lasted a short time because the planet's high temperature and pressure destroyed it. Our probes are much more

capable of surviving on Venus's surface. They will take temperature and pressure measurements, but they'll also take pictures and video."

"What's a probe?" Cozzie asked.

"It's like a small spaceship we'll send to Venus to collect scientific information," Yasmin said.

"What's pressure?" he asked.

"It's kind of hard to describe," I said.

"Cozzie, on Earth, air pressure is the force of the atmosphere pressing down on us," Lin added. I felt as if he was trying to show off.

"On Venus, the pressure is much more than on Earth," Yasmin interrupted.

It was as if Yasmin and Lin were in a knowledge duel.

"How can we help?" I asked, trying to move the conversation forward.

Mum said, "We're going to orbit the planet, and as we do, you'll take turns releasing probes into the atmosphere. Follow me."

We followed Mum to meet Professor Will. He was waiting for us in the tech pod. Professor Will is always building or fixing something.

"I've been excited about this mission for so long I can't even believe the day has finally arrived," he said. "For thousands of years, people have wondered what's under the clouds of Venus. Less than one hundred years ago, some people thought it was like a jungle full of lush plants and wild animals."

"Is it?" Cozzie asked.

"No," Lin answered. "It's a baking-hot wasteland. Nothing can survive there."

"Its pressure and lack of oxygen make life there impossible," Yasmin added.

Mum seemed impressed with their knowledge of Venus. She wasn't picking up on the fact that they were just trying to outdo each other.

Cozzie looked disappointed. "Why are we going to visit somewhere we can't explore?"

"We want to learn more," Mum answered. "Venus is hidden beneath those mysterious clouds. I want to find out what's down there."

"You're not alone," Professor Will said. "Now who wants to drop the first probe?"

"Me!" Apollo said, stepping forward right away. I could tell that Mum was a bit embarrassed, because she had talked to us a million times about letting the guests go first and making the experience about them.

"Why don't we let Lin or Yasmin go first?" I suggested.

"I've been looking forward to this, Starr," Apollo said, not catching my drift.

"I agree with Starr," Mum said.

Yasmin and Lin tossed a coin to decide, and Yasmin won. Yasmin floated forwards, looking proud.

"All right, young lady," Professor Will said. "You're about to become the first human to ever drop a probe while orbiting Venus!"

"Awesome!" she exclaimed. "What do I have to do?"

"You're going to pull that lever," he said, pointing to something that reminded me of the gear stick on Dad's old car on Earth. "A probe will be released from the bottom of our space station. With our stunning view through the clear pod walls, we'll actually be able to watch as the probe plunges into the clouds below. If I did my job right, the probe will fall through the atmosphere and start sending back video and scientific data."

"Let's do it!" Yasmin declared.

I looked at Lin. He did not look happy. He was pouting over Yasmin getting to go first.

We turned our attention to Venus below. I couldn't wait to have a look at what was going on under those clouds.

"How do I know when to drop it?" she asked.

"Trust yourself," he said. "Since we can't see the surface through the clouds, we're going to drop many probes. Where they end up depends on you."

"Sounds good to me," Yasmin said. "3, 2, 1, DROP!"

SPACE VOLLEYBALL

We took turns at pulling the lever and dropping the probes. The lights on the probes blinked as they fell towards the clouds and then vanished on their way to the surface of Venus. Mum and Professor Will said that they would let us know once they had some data back from the probes.

The other kids and I all cruised back to the leisure pod. We had been playing a lot of microgravity volleyball on the trip out to Venus. It was fun and helped to pass the time.

Volleyball in microgravity is quite different from on Earth. For instance, the ball moves much slower and you're floating. Yasmin and I were playing together against Lin and Apollo. I thought this was a little unfair because they were older, but Yasmin really wanted to try to beat them. I was just trying to have some fun.

Yasmin served the ball and it slowly sailed over the net, which was about twice the height as it is on Earth. Lin jumped up and floated to meet the ball. He hit it hard back over the net, sending it to the bottom of the pod and earning a point. Yasmin floated in close to me and hissed, "You've got to get those shots!"

I was surprised that she had become so upset. "That was a really good play, Lin," I said, trying to be positive.

"You know we're trying to beat them . . . right?" Yasmin said to me sarcastically.

I couldn't believe she was taking it so seriously. "Of course I do," I said, trying to shake it off.

"Well, then act like it," she said rudely.

"Come on, stop talking! We're ready to serve!" Apollo called. I could tell he hadn't heard what Yasmin said.

Lin served the ball. Yasmin tipped the ball back to the other side. Lin hit it hard at me again. I managed to get a hand on it, but it didn't go over the net.

"Seriously?" Yasmin asked under her breath.

I didn't say anything. The rest of the game didn't get any better. Yasmin kept saying nasty things, but she did it in a way that Apollo couldn't hear. I even tried playing closer to the net, thinking that he might hear her then, but it didn't work.

I was relieved when the game was over. Yasmin and Lin went back to their pods to meet their parents. Apollo and I cruised to meet the rest of the family.

"Did you hear any of that?" I asked, zipping in close to him and his cruiser.

"Hear any of what?" he asked.

"The way Yasmin was talking to me during the game. She was being really mean."

"I didn't hear her being mean," he said. "Are you sure you're not just mad that you lost?"

"I don't care that we lost," I replied. "I'm telling you, she was putting me down under her breath the whole game and blaming *me* every time we lost a point."

We were still talking as we cruised into the family pod. Dad was working on his video equipment, Cozzie was juggling three coloured balls and Mum was on the computer.

"Congratulations! Your probes have just started to send back data," Mum said, smiling. "Professor Will should have the information ready for you by the morning."

Apollo and I floated over to Mum to have a look. Numbers and symbols covered her computer screen. "What do you have so far?" I asked.

"Well, Venus is hot," Mum replied. "We knew that already. But it seems to have different temperatures in different places. The probes will help us decide the best possible place for us to explore more."

"Starr hates Yasmin," Apollo said suddenly.

"That's not true," I replied, turning to him. "I just don't think she's very nice."

"Starr!" Mum scolded. "Yasmin and her family are our guests. You can't talk like that. *It's* not nice."

"*She's* not nice, Mum. You haven't heard the way she talks to me when no one else is around."

"I haven't heard anything," Apollo said.

"Yasmin is a very nice girl," Mum said. "Maybe it's just that you've been cooped up in this space station for the last few weeks and you're getting on each other's nerves."

I wanted to tell Mum what I really thought – that it was probably only going to get worse – but I didn't. "We'll see," I said instead.

Chapter 3

TOASTED MARSHMALLOWS

The next morning, Professor Will called the kids back to the tech pod.

"Good news," he said. "Since the probes you dropped yesterday are working so well, we'll drop more today."

One at a time, we took turns at pulling the lever and dropping the remaining probes. "The way the probes vanish into the thick clouds reminds me of a cherry falling through a milkshake," Lin said.

"I could go for a milkshake," Cozzie said, rubbing his belly.

"I wonder what it will be like on the surface," I said.

"The surface of a milkshake is very cold," Cozzie said.

"Not the milkshake, silly," I said, smiling.

"It's going to be really hot. *Everyone* knows that," Yasmin said and rolled her eyes. It was quick and no one else noticed it. I saw it, though. It's weird how something as small as an eye roll can hurt your feelings, but it did.

"I'll be right back," Professor Will said. "I need to run a few things through my computers."

Apollo was on his phone again, and Cozzie was looking over Apollo's shoulder and watching whatever he was doing.

I tried not to let what Yasmin had done bother me. "I wonder *how* hot the surface is," I said.

I watched her closely, but she didn't roll her eyes again.

Lin said, "We know it will be around 430 degrees Celsius because of the measurements taken from other probes in the past."

"Anyone who knows anything about Venus should at least know that," Yasmin said. Yasmin and Lin looked at each other and smirked. Lin shook his head from side to side in disbelief. They were making fun of me!

"You know, some scientists believe the best place to build a colony on Venus is in the clouds," I said.

"Sure," Lin said.

"Whatever you say," Yasmin added.

I didn't know what to say. I was right. I'd read about it.

"I wonder if it's hot enough to bake cookies," Cozzie wondered out loud, rejoining the conversation.

"You'd burn your cookies down there," Lin said. The way he said it was nicer.

"I'd like to toast some marshmallows on one of those volcanoes they have on Venus," Apollo said, putting his phone away.

I felt kind of embarrassed by what Apollo said. Apollo had been given the same training as all of us before going on the journey to Venus, but it was clear that he

wasn't taking it very seriously.

I replied, "We can't toast marshmallows over a volcano. We probably aren't even going to go to the surface. It's too hot."

"We have to go to the surface," Apollo said. "Why else would Mum have brought us all the way out here?"

"We hope to go to the surface, but the heat might be too much for us to survive," I said.

"It's not just because of the heat," Lin said. "It's the pressure that is the most difficult thing to figure out. It would crush you in an instant. I can't believe you don't know that."

I looked at Apollo, hoping for some help. He was playing with his phone again. Even though Apollo and I were in charge of our team, it didn't feel that way.

"Venus presents many problems," Professor Will said, returning from his computer. "We certainly have our work cut out for us."

"I think we can do it," Cozzie said confidently.

My phone buzzed. It was a video call from Tia. "Hey, are you looking at the data from the probes you dropped?" she asked, almost as soon as I answered.

"We're just getting it back now," I said.

"The data shows if we were to go to Venus without protection, we'd catch fire, be crushed instantly and have nothing to breathe," Tia said. "I don't see how a human can go to the surface and come back alive."

Cozzie looked terrified. I felt bad for him in that moment. He was only five. I could tell all the talk about Venus was making him nervous.

Meanwhile, Professor Will clicked away on his computer.

"Can we have a look at the data too?" Lin asked.

"Of course," Professor Will said, pointing to another computer. "Starr, if you log in to that computer over there, you'll be able to see some of the data from your probes."

"I'm going to get something to eat and then head back to my pod," Apollo said.

"But we're about to see the first data from our probes," I reminded him. "Don't you want to see what they find?"

"I'll see it later. Right now, I need to discover something to eat," he said.

I watched Apollo take off and leave me on my own with Yasmin and Lin.

I logged on to the computer, but couldn't get the data from our probes to display. Professor Will had to stop what he was doing to come over and help me. I noticed them sniggering about it. I looked to Professor Will, but he was too focused to notice. *But I haven't done anything to them*, I thought.

I kept replaying the moment in my mind throughout the rest of the day. Later on, I called Allison.

"They're probably not realizing how much it's hurting your feelings," she said. "You need to tell them how it's hurting you and that you want them to stop."

"It's not that easy," I said.

"Of course it is," she said. "If someone is hurting your

feelings, you should tell them how it's making you feel. If they're your friends, they'll stop."

"That's the thing," I said. "I don't think they want to be my friends."

Chapter 4

DISTANT STARR

As soon as I hung up with Allison, Tia called. We talked on a video call for a little while before she asked, "What's wrong?"

"Lin and Yasmin are being really weird," I said.

"Weird how?" she asked.

"It's like they're showing off how much they know about Venus. It's kind of annoying."

"Why doesn't your mum say something?"

"I don't think she sees it," I replied. "She thinks they're just sharing ideas, but I know they're really showing off."

"Are you sure?" she asked. "They seemed fine during training. They're always really nice to me."

"I'm telling you. All they care about is being the smartest."

"Why don't you talk to them about it?"

"I can't do that," I said. "They'll just find a way to make me look foolish."

"Maybe. I guess there's only one way to find out," she said, turning her attention back to her computer. "In other news, have you seen the data coming back from the probes?"

Tia did have the habit of changing subjects quickly. She was funny like that.

"I was having trouble logging in earlier. I haven't seen much yet," I said.

"You've got to check it out. There are lots of pictures and even some videos coming in. Venus is one strange place. You should go back and check the data. You're in charge, you know. Don't let them push you around."

“I’m just not sure how to lead a team when the people on the team don’t like me,” I replied.

Tia’s attention had shifted completely to the computer screen. She didn’t respond.

I ended the call and cruised off to find my dad. He was usually good in situations like this.

When I found him, he had just come back from a space walk. He does them often to get video of the outside of the ship. I’d gone with him a few times before. When we lived on Earth, we used to go for walks all the time. Space walks were just like our normal walks on Earth, but with protective equipment and floating in space.

“Hey, sweetie,” Dad said, taking off his helmet.

“How was your space walk?” I asked.

“Miraculous!” he exclaimed. “I shot some great video of Venus. It’s an unbelievable view from out there.”

“That’s great,” I said. I couldn’t bring myself to tell Dad about Yasmin and Lin. I wanted to. I knew telling him was the right thing to do and that he’d probably have a way to help. But when I started telling Dad, I had second thoughts.

"Everything okay?" he asked. "You seem a bit distant, Starr. Get it?"

That is one of Dad's favourite lines when he knows something is bothering me.

"Yes, very funny," I replied. "I'm fine, just missing home, I guess."

"That's understandable," he said. "Have you talked with Allison and Tia lately? It's important for you to stay connected with your friends on Earth."

"Yes, it's just . . . I guess I'm just missing them."

"How about we go on a space walk tomorrow?" he asked. "You've been cooped up in the station for days. You need to get out and get . . . I was about to say some fresh air, but there isn't any air! So, you should just get out. It's good for you."

I smiled. Maybe Dad was right. A space walk might

be just what I needed. “Okay,” I said. “I’ll meet you tomorrow.”

“Great! Let’s do it in the morning. Bring Lin and Yasmin too,” Dad said. I cringed a little. I hadn’t wanted to go with them, just Dad.

“I think they’re busy in the morning tomorrow,” I said.

“Ask them,” he replied.

I cruised back to find the rest of the kids. I took the long way around the station. The way the sunlight hit Venus made the clouds look like an orange swirl. The more I looked at it, the more curious I became about what was on the surface under the clouds.

I zoomed through the tech pod, and then Professor Will waved me over. “What’s up?” I asked.

“Images and video are coming in like crazy,” he said. “You’ve got to have a look.”

I looked at his computer screen. It was the clearest image of Venus’s surface I’d ever seen. “Wow!” I gasped.

The image showed it to be a rocky, hazy place. Rocks

were everywhere and small mountains were in the distance. "Is this the only one?" I asked.

He smiled. "This is one of thousands. Our little probe project just rocketed the human study of Venus light years ahead."

"How did the probes hold up in the high temperatures?" I asked.

"Starr," he said. "I built them with my own two hands. How do you think they're holding up?"

I smiled. "Awesomely?" I asked.

"Of course. Let's just say it's a good thing I know a lot about composite metals. You know, mixing the right combination of metals."

"What other information can it give us? How hot it is down there, for example?" I asked.

"It depends where you are, but on the surface, for the probe that I'm linked with now, it's 453 degrees Celsius."

"Don't we bake cakes at 180 degrees Celsius?" I asked.

"I'm not much of a baker, but yes, that sounds about

right. It's about two and a half times the temperature needed to bake a cake."

"Is there any way people can live on the surface?" I asked.

"I have a few ideas. I'm going to test them later today if you want to stop by and help out."

"I'd love to," I said.

Chapter 5

PHASE TWO

After lunch, the professor invited the kids to the tech pod to see his latest work. We gathered in front of him and he said, “I built a Venus simulator using the data that’s come back from the probes.” He was pointing to one of his inventions, about the size of a refrigerator. Its doors were as clear as glass so you could see inside easily.

“Are we going in there?” Cozzie asked.

“No, but we are going to put in some familiar objects and see how they hold up,” he continued. “We’ve talked about the three main challenges to surviving on the

surface of Venus. They are high heat, high pressure and lack of oxygen. This simulator creates conditions very similar to the ones we'd encounter on the surface."

Professor Will turned to Apollo. "Please take this metal container and place it inside the simulator," the professor said.

Apollo placed it inside. He closed the door and floated back towards Professor Will.

"So we know the temperature on Venus is well over 430 degrees Celsius and the pressure is about ten times more than on Earth," the professor said. "Let's see what would happen if you put a simple metal can on the surface." He floated over to his laptop.

I caught the professor's eye. "Starr, would you like to start the experiment?" he asked. I nodded and floated over to where he stood.

He told me to press a button, and when I did, the metal can didn't really catch fire and it didn't really boil. It did something I'd never seen before. It crumpled up like it had been crushed, and then it vanished.

"Anyone like to guess what just happened to the can?" Professor Will asked.

"The pressure crushed it," Lin said.

"Then the intense heat melted it and turned it to vapour," Yasmin interrupted.

"You're right," the professor replied. "It's really hard to predict how something is going to behave in an environment like that."

We made a list of other items we wanted to test in the simulator. We tested different kinds of metals, cloth and rubber. Everything was destroyed almost instantly. It was frightening.

"Well," Professor Will said after a few trials, "what are your thoughts after watching the way materials behave in Venus's atmosphere?"

"I think I want to go back to Earth," Cozzie said.

Professor Will grinned and said, "That's a logical response, Cozzie. But our mission is to gather information about Venus and try to visit the surface. Anyone have any ideas as to how we can do that?"

"The intense pressure reminds me of the deep oceans on Earth," I said. "I've seen videos of scientists searching deep in the ocean for sunken ships and new sea life. In the videos, the scientists are always in submarines. If they weren't, the pressure of all that water would crush them."

"Being on the surface of Venus is a lot like being deep in the ocean on Earth," Professor Will said.

Mum cruised in as Professor Will was talking. He stopped and she said, "The video and pictures we've collected are crystal clear and better than we'd imagined. Based on the temperature and pressure readings, I think we might be ready for phase two."

"Does it involve lava-surfing down a volcano?" asked Apollo.

Everyone looked at Apollo in disbelief.

"No, we won't be surfing on a volcano," Mum said.

"Awww," Apollo replied.

"In phase two, you're each going to get a remote-controlled vehicle to explore the surface," Mum said.

"We think that the remotes will be able to survive on Venus's surface," said Professor Will. "They're made of the same materials as the probes, and the probes seem to be holding up fine."

"Awesome!" Yasmin and Lin said at the same time.

Yasmin even tried to high five me. I didn't hold my hand up to meet hers. Mum noticed, and I could tell she was annoyed. Yasmin played it up as if her feelings were hurt.

I couldn't figure Yasmin out. One minute she was mean to me, and then the next she's giving me a high five and acting like we're best friends. The only things I knew for certain were that I was excited to use the remotes and that Mum was mad at me.

Chapter 6

KNOW-IT-ALLS

"What's going on between you and Yasmin?" Mum asked later that night in our living room pod.

"You're not seeing it, Mum," I said. "Yasmin and Lin aren't very nice."

"Starr, what I saw today was clearly you not being nice to her," Mum sighed. "The poor girl tried to high five you and you practically turned away from her. We're all supposed to be on the same team here. You're one of the team leaders, for goodness sake."

I didn't know what to say. No matter what I replied,

I was going to be in trouble with Mum. She was convinced that I was the problem. I was a little upset that she didn't believe me. She is *my* mum after all. She should have been on my side, not Yasmin's. I decided it wasn't worth trying to explain it to her, so I said, "You're right. I shouldn't have done that today. It won't happen again."

"We're going to have to work as a team if we're to succeed," she said.

"I know," I said. The way Dad was looking at me, I could tell that he knew something more was going on.

Later that night, when he tucked me in, he said, "Why did you apologize earlier? I could tell you didn't really mean it."

"Mum doesn't believe that Lin and Yasmin are being difficult. All she sees is that I'm being mean to them. I'm not, though."

"I know you well enough to know that something weird is going on. What exactly are they doing that's so bad?"

"It's hard to explain," I said.

"Keep doing what you're doing," Dad said. "Be nice to them and focus on the mission. If they keep making bad choices, Mum will see it sooner or later and know you were telling the truth."

"Can you talk to her for me?" I asked.

"I think the best thing to do right now is to focus on the mission. Everything else will work itself out. More importantly, are we still on for that space walk tomorrow morning?"

"Definitely," I answered.

"Remember to include Lin and Yasmin. Maybe things will be better with them tomorrow."

"I'll invite them, but you'll see. They're going to be mean to me."

I slept like a rock that night. In the morning, I couldn't wait to get out and go on the space walk with Dad. I wasn't crazy about including Yasmin and Lin, but I had no choice. I floated out of my bed and noticed that I'd

missed a few calls. I checked and saw that they were from Allison and Tia.

I called them back on a group call. Allison answered first. Her face appeared on the screen. "Good morning," she said.

"What time is it?" I asked.

"It's ten in the morning here in Colorado."

"Wow! I really slept late," I said as Tia joined the call.

We said hello, and then Tia said, "Starr, the video from the probes is fascinating! I can't believe you are going to be using remote vehicles on the surface."

"I know. I'm really excited," I said. "I'll have to make this call quick because I'm supposed to meet my Dad in a little while for a space walk."

"Are things better with Lin and Yasmin?" Allison asked.

"Nope! Now Mum thinks I'm the mean one."

"What about your dad?" Tia asked.

"We're going on a space walk in a little while and he told me to invite them."

"That's perfect," Allison said. "He'll see how they're behaving and know you're telling the truth."

"I hope so," I said.

After the call, I got dressed and headed off on my cruiser to get Yasmin and Lin. I found them at breakfast.

I floated over to where they were seated and strapped in next to them. "Do you want to go on a space walk with my dad and me?" I asked reluctantly.

Their eyes bulged.

"Yes!" Lin said.

"I'd love to!" Yasmin added.

I had a feeling they were being nice just to go on the walk. It felt kind of fake.

I knew inviting them was the right thing to do. But I really wished Dad hadn't made me. They were already acting nice just so they could go. "I'll see you later. Meet Dad and me at the tech pod in twenty minutes."

After breakfast, I cruised to the tech pod to meet Dad. I was hoping they wouldn't show up, but I then remembered how excited they were so, of course, they had arrived before me.

As I pulled in with my cruiser, Yasmin and Lin both waved. I made my way over to them and Professor Will. Dad cruised in right after me. In no time at all we were suited up and ready to take a leap out into space.

I stood next to Dad, preparing for Professor Will to open the exit hatch.

"They're just pretending to be nice," I whispered.

He leaned in close and said, "Starr, focus on what is happening right now. We're orbiting Venus! Be present and in the moment!"

We put on our helmets. I was careful not to say anything else because the helmets had microphones that allowed us all to hear each other.

Standing there, I realized I had lost my focus over the last few days. I had let the nonsense going on with Yasmin and Lin distract me from the fact that we were the only humans to ever orbit Venus. I tried to relax as

Dad stepped out into space holding my hand. Yasmin and Lin followed right behind us.

Chapter 7

ATTACK!

When I've looked down on Earth during other space walks, I've seen the beautiful blues, greens and browns of the water and land. Venus's surface was completely hidden by clouds.

"I wonder what's going on down there," I said.

"I can't wait to check it out with the remote vehicles," Lin said. "I think we're going to find active volcanos."

"Me too," Yasmin added.

Lin said, "I'm curious about what's going on *in* the clouds. Did you know that some scientists think that the best place for humans to live on Venus would be in the clouds?"

"I told you that the other day," I reminded him.

"I don't remember that," he said.

"It's not important who said it first, Starr," Yasmin said. "You don't have to get upset."

"I'm not getting upset!" I said, suddenly sounding really upset.

"Starr," Dad interrupted. "It's really not important who said it first. Many scientists believe we could build floating cities in the clouds."

"I've read about the idea before," Yasmin said with a smirk. I caught it, but Dad missed it.

I could tell by the look on Dad's face that he thought I was being difficult.

"I'm just saying that I'm the one who mentioned that idea to them," I said. I wasn't helping make my case that Yasmin and Lin were being mean to me.

The space walk hadn't gone how I planned. When we

were back inside, I tried to talk to Dad about it, but he said he'd heard enough from me.

I was feeling rubbish when we met up with Professor Will, Mum and a group of scientists from the crew at the tech pod. They were ready for us to launch the remotes. Mum and Dad talked privately for a few minutes, and I knew he told her about what had happened. Mum looked disappointed.

Before I had a chance to talk with her, the professor said, "Each of you is going to have a remote-controlled vehicle to explore the surface and the clouds. It's capable of rolling, flying and even digging into the surface to take samples. The vehicles are about as indestructible as possible, but please be as careful as you can."

"The remotes are fitted with high-resolution cameras," Mum said. "You'll control them from the safety of the tech pod."

"Please be careful not to crash into each other or any of the other remotes we'll have down there," Professor

Will added. "Several of the crew members are also guiding remote vehicles."

"How many remotes will be flying?" Lin asked.

"A total of ten," the professor said.

"It's like we're attacking Venus," Apollo said.

"Not exactly," Mum said. "But we're definitely sending more vehicles to Venus than ever before. We'll learn more about Venus in the next few hours than we have learned in all of human history."

"Cozzie is going to count down from ten, and then you'll be ready to explore," Dad said.

We all put on our headsets and strapped into chairs to keep us from floating around. The headset had a visor that covered my eyes completely. It was like the ultimate video game. In my visor I could see the view from the front of my vehicle. The video was crystal clear and made me feel as if I were sitting in the vehicle myself.

I could also control my view from several different cameras mounted in the remote. With the click of a

button I was able switch between the cameras, giving me views from all sides.

Cozzie said, "Drivers ready! ATTACK!!!"

Even though I was feeling fed up, I couldn't help but laugh. Cozzie always seems to cheer me up. I let my vehicle fall, and for the first time all day, I was having fun. The sensation reminded me of those movies where you're in a special cinema seat that moves around. I had seen one at Disney a few years before.

My stomach lurched, making me feel like I was falling, so I pressed the "Lift" button and the vehicle slowed down a little. I looked to my left and saw the other vehicles racing for the clouds. I decided to explore above the clouds on my own for a little while.

Then, slowly and carefully, I lowered the vehicle into the clouds.

The wind picked up right away. The wind speed and the temperature appeared on my screen. It was getting hot and the wind was blowing like crazy. I was surprised that the remote stayed on course and didn't flip over or become hard to control.

Once in the clouds, my view vanished. The clouds weren't like the clouds on Earth. They had an eerie orange colour. It gave me a creepy feeling and I said, "Anyone out there?"

"Yeah," Apollo said. "This is awesome!"

"It's creeping me out. I'm so glad we're not actually down there," I said.

"I can't see anything yet," Lin said. "The clouds are so thick."

"I just dropped out of the clouds," Yasmin said. "You've got to see this!"

Chapter 8

ALIENS!

By the time my vehicle dropped below the clouds, I saw that everyone else's vehicles were there too.

At first I couldn't make out too much detail, since we were still so high, but it was clear there was nothing living on Venus. It looked like a massive rocky desert stretching out in all directions. The sky had an orange-sunset look to it.

"This is so weird," Lin said. "I keep waiting to see something green or blue, but there's no life here and definitely no water."

I continued to lower towards the surface. "Hey," I said, "the lower I go, the slower the wind gets."

"I'm still way up high and the winds are hurricane level," Yasmin said. "But you're right. The winds are stronger in the higher atmosphere and very slow on the surface."

"The winds are far stronger than any hurricane on Earth," Lin replied.

"There's almost no wind on the surface," I said. "I'm going to try to land."

"Be careful," I heard a voice that sounded like Tia say. "Try setting it down over there by those flat rocks."

"Tia?" I asked.

"Yes?" asked Tia.

"Where are you?" I replied.

"I'm on Earth, of course, at the training centre. I'm watching a live feed of your video stream and I'm linked in to your conversation."

"Cool," I said. I was really thankful that Professor

Will's equipment worked so well and kept me connected to people on Earth.

I lowered the vehicle to the surface and then it basically landed itself. Once on the ground, I took a deep breath. I think I might have forgotten to breathe for a few minutes on the way down. Even though my body was safe and comfortable in the space station, my heart raced like crazy.

"It's like a volcanic wasteland," Tia said.

She was right. It's weird to think of a planet the size of Earth being completely free of life. Earth is packed with billions and billions of living things. "There's nothing here," I said. "It's a little sad."

"Are you kidding?" Yasmin asked. "This is the most beautiful thing I've ever seen."

I didn't say it wasn't beautiful, I thought. "It's beautiful, but there's nothing here," I said, defending myself.

"I just found something," Apollo said.

"What is it?" I asked.

"I can't believe my eyes. This is the craziest thing ever!"

"What is it?" Lin asked.

"I found some kind of life form. It's looking right at me."

He couldn't be serious. "No way!" I said.

"I'm not kidding. I'm looking right at it."

"What is it?" Yasmin asked.

"It's green. It's about my height. I've never seen anything like it before."

No one said anything.

"Oh no! There are more."

We all waited to see what he would say next.

"I'm looking at your video stream, and I don't see anything," Tia said.

"You're not looking close enough," Apollo said, panicked. "There are hundreds of them. ALIENS! They're eating my brain!"

VENUS HOLIDAY

"You can't mess around like that," Mum said.

"How could anyone believe that aliens were eating my brain?" Apollo asked. "I was sitting next to you all on the station."

"You scared the other kids. You also panicked the crew," Mum replied.

"I'm sorry," Apollo said. "It was kind of funny, though, don't you think?"

"Not even a little bit," Mum said.

I was trying my best not to laugh. It *was* kind of

funny, though. Apollo was wrong to pretend that he had seen aliens. He was sitting right next to me, so I had been quite sure aliens weren't eating him. The part that wasn't cool was the fact that Cozzie is afraid of aliens. Apollo knows that and did the joke anyway.

That night I couldn't stop thinking about the surface of Venus. It was such a strange place. I kept thinking about my vehicle, parked on the surface, waiting for me to power it up and explore some more.

The next day, the whole crew aboard the station met to talk more about the things we'd seen on the surface. Mrs Sosa and Tia were connected with us by videoconference. Mrs Sosa addressed the group.

"Congratulations!" she said to the crew. "Yesterday you all pushed our understanding of Venus to the next level. The images and video that we have are absolutely miraculous."

"Now that we've proven that our remote vehicles can handle the atmosphere on Venus," Mum said, "the

challenge is to find out if there is a way to set up a permanent station on Venus. Some say that the surface is far too dangerous and a floating city in the clouds is the only real possibility. The main problem with a cloud colony is that the wind is extraordinarily strong."

"In the end, the answer might be that there is no way to build a permanent station on Venus," said Professor Will.

"Kids, do you think humans are capable of surviving on Venus?" Mrs Sosa asked.

"I think we could find a way to survive there. Especially now that we know that the remotes and probes can handle the environment," Lin said.

"The biggest challenge seems to be how we'd manage to eat and have drinking water," Yasmin added.

I had to admit, Lin and Yasmin knew their stuff. Oddly, it made me feel really frustrated for some reason.

"You're right. So far, everything has gone better than we planned," said Mrs Sosa. "The probes worked, the remote vehicles worked and now we're confident enough that we're going to send you all to the surface. You'll stay one day on the surface and one day in the clouds. Congratulations, you're about to become the first colonists of Venus!"

Chapter 10

MINI STATION

What do you pack when you're spending a few days on the heat-baked surface of Venus or in its poisonous clouds? I had no idea. So I brought my cuddly toys and sweets. *Lots* of sweets.

"How do you know we're going to be able to survive down there?" I asked Mum. We were on a space walk with the professor to prepare some of the pods for a landing on Venus. The main station was made up of more than fifty pods. We were going to detach seven of them to create a mini station.

"The seven pods that we'll bring down to Venus are built from the same materials as the probes and remotes. We know they'll be able to stand up to the temperatures and pressures on the surface."

Professor Will asked me to press a few buttons on a small computer tablet. "This program will cause the pods that we're taking to Venus to disconnect from the main station," he said. We watched as one of the tubes connecting the pods to the main station disconnected. A cluster of seven pods slowly floated away from the main station.

"These pods will be able to handle anything Venus can throw at them," Professor Will said.

Mum took out her tablet and started typing more computer code. Each string of code told the pods or the tubes to move in different ways. Within twenty minutes, Mum had programmed the pods to form the shape of a small ship. I was so impressed by how fast she was able to do it.

"That's unbelievable," I said.

The three of us took the mini station for a spin to test it out. Mum steered the station, while the professor gave the pods a final safety inspection.

"Things seem to have got better with Yasmin and Lin," Mum said.

"I guess," I replied. "It's just been really hard working with them."

"You know, when I was a little girl, I was very smart like you," Mum said. "Sometimes the other kids gave me a hard time because of it."

"That's not what's happening, Mum. If anything, they're treating me badly because I'm not smart enough. They think I'm stupid."

"Starr, don't say that."

"It's how I feel," I said. "They know everything there is to know about Venus and I don't." Suddenly I was feeling really upset, which surprised me. I hadn't seen it coming.

"Just because you don't know everything about Venus

doesn't mean you're not smart," Mum replied.

We cruised back to the main station. "You don't see it, but they're not very nice to me. It's all right. I don't mind because they're going to be gone soon enough when the trip is over."

"It does matter," Mum said. "If they aren't being nice you have the right to say something. There's always a solution if you look hard enough for it. You shouldn't let other people ruin your experience."

Mum was right, and for the first time I felt as if she believed me. "So what do I do?" I asked.

"It's hard to know that until the moment presents itself."

Chapter 11

CLOUD CITIES

Part of me felt as though we were going on some kind of new ride at an amusement park. Another part of me knew that this trip down to the surface of Venus was real. Mum steered the mini station above the clouds, looking for a good place to drop in.

"The interesting things about the clouds," said Mum, "are the pressure and temperature. We've located a layer in the clouds where the pressure is close to that on Earth and the temperature isn't too hot. I'm going to that spot first."

We dropped into the clouds, and then everything turned a dirty white. Wind howled against the outside of the ship. It was a weird experience because there really wasn't anything to see.

"How can a ship in the clouds survive long-term?" Lin asked. "I mean, wouldn't you have to hover in the clouds and burn fuel non-stop?"

"That's a good question," Mum said. "No, we'll use a balloon to stay afloat, like this one."

She pressed a button and a gigantic balloon opened and filled above the ship. It was like the most amazing magic trick of all time. In fact, it was less like a hot-air balloon and more like a mini blimp attached to the top of the ship.

It changed from feeling as if we were flying to feeling as if we were floating.

"We're not relying on fuel right now. We're simply floating in the cloud layer," Professor Will said.

"This is amazing!" Cozzie shouted.

It was amazing. We *were* one of the clouds of Venus at that moment. Everyone was very excited. Suddenly, the bickering with Yasmin and Lin seemed really foolish to me and I wondered how it had got so bad.

"We're going to spend the night here and experience life on Venus, I mean . . . above Venus," Mum said. "I suggest you settle in and enjoy the ride. We'll only have one day here, and then tomorrow we're heading to the surface for the last day of our mission."

Apollo, who had been looking at his phone, said, "Actually, there really isn't a *tomorrow* on Venus for months and months because the length of one day on Venus is 243 Earth days."

"I didn't realize you were so informed about Venus," Mum said.

"I'm a colonist now," Apollo said. "The least I can do is know a thing or two about the place. Also, with all the arguing Yasmin, Lin and Starr have been doing on this trip, I've had plenty of time to read about Venus."

"I thought you were playing games on your phone all this time," I said.

"No, it's called research. You should try it," he said sarcastically.

"Also, is a day here actually 243 Earth days?" I asked.

"Yes!" Lin and Yasmin said at the same time. They continued talking about the difference between a day and a year on Venus, but I couldn't listen anymore. It became really clear to me that we'd been the foolish ones since arriving on Venus. Yasmin and Lin had spent much of their time trying to outdo each other and show off. I'd spent too much of my time worrying about how they treated me.

"Stop!" I shouted. I hadn't meant for it to come out as a shout, but it did. Everyone stopped talking and looked at me. I turned to face Yasmin and Lin. "I get it. You're both really smart and know just about everything there is to know about Venus. But you don't have to keep trying to outdo each other all the time."

Mum looked as if she might say something, but she didn't. Yasmin and Lin looked a little upset.

"You were selected for this trip because you love Venus so much," I added.

"I do love Venus," Yasmin said.

"It's the most fascinating planet in the solar system," Lin added.

"I think you have been so focused on trying to show how much you know that you haven't been focused on the fact that we're *really* here."

"I don't know why," Lin said, "but I've felt like I had to keep showing that I deserved to be on this trip. It seemed too good to be true."

"Me too," Yasmin added. "I was afraid that everyone on the station would be smarter than me – especially you, Starr."

"Me?" I asked.

"Yeah," Lin said. "You've been all over the solar system."

"You're like a super astronaut," Yasmin added.

Mum looked at me, smiled and shrugged. They were being so honest with me that I thought it was time I did the same.

"The weird thing is I've been feeling really intimidated by you both," I admitted. I told them how it hurt my feelings when they were mean to me. They told me how intimidated they'd felt about being on the trip. For the first time on the trip, I felt as if we were a team.

"Apollo, do you have anything you want to say?" Mum asked.

"Not really," he said.

"Tell us more about how long a day on Venus is," Cozzie said.

"Well, a day on Venus is longer than a year," Apollo replied. "It takes Venus 243 Earth days to turn just one time. So one day on Venus is actually 243 Earth days. A year – the time it takes Venus to orbit the Sun – takes about 225 Earth days. So, on Venus a day is longer than a year."

"A day isn't longer than a year," Cozzie said, sounding a little argumentative.

"See what all your bickering has done to Cozzie?" Dad said.

I did see what he meant. Cozzie was usually very agreeable and easy to get along with. "Cozzie, I'm sorry you've had to watch the three of us having such a hard time getting along," I said.

"Yeah," Yasmin said. "We should be working together, not trying to prove each other wrong."

"I say we start right now," Lin said. "I don't know about you, but this is a dream come true for me." He pointed up above the ship to the balloon floating us in Venus's clouds.

"We're finally ready to work as a team," I said to Mum.

"And not a moment too soon," she said. "Let's get your computers and start taking a closer look at the measurements we're getting from your probes. Work together and see if there's a place you think we should land on the surface tomorrow. We're trying to determine if there are active lava flows happening on Venus."

"You mean today?" Apollo asked. "It won't be tomorrow for about 200 days."

"Yes . . . I guess I do," Mum said.

We spent the next few hours looking at the images, video and temperature readings coming back from our probes. It had taken almost the entire mission to learn to get along, but it felt awesome to finally be working together.

Towards the end of that first Earth day, we gave our recommendation to Mum about where we felt we could safely land the ship on the surface. We all agreed on a spot in the middle of a range containing hundreds of volcanoes.

That night, all the kids camped out in the same pod and had a sleepover. It's not every day you get to have a sleepover while floating in the clouds of Venus. It was magical and something I won't forget if I live to be one hundred years old. It was hard to imagine we'd had such a difficult time getting along throughout the trip.

When we woke, Mum didn't waste any time. She released the balloon that had been keeping us afloat and switched back to rocket power. Then she steered us down, out of the clouds. We flew for almost an hour until we came to the spot we'd selected.

Volcanoes stretched out as far as the eye could see. She landed the ship in an area between two high volcanoes. Once on the ground, she said, "We'll spend one more Earth day in this location. We won't be able to leave the ship, the pressure is too great, but you can use your remotes and explore the area."

We spent the day zipping and zooming around the surface of Venus and checking out all the volcanoes. Apollo was convinced we'd find one that was active and had flowing lava. We knew there might be one out there somewhere. If it was out there, I knew we were going to find it.

I thought about all the incredible places I'd already been in the solar system and all the unbelievable things I'd seen. Then I thought about the rest of the solar system and imagined all the places waiting to be discovered. *I might be a normal girl,* I thought, *but my life is completely out of this world!*

ABOUT THE AUTHOR

Raymond Bean is the best-selling author of the *Benji Franklin, Sweet Farts* and *School Is a Nightmare* books. He teaches by day and writes by night. He lives in New York, USA with his wife, two children and a Cockapoo called Lily. His bags are packed for the day when space holidays become a reality.

ABOUT THE ILLUSTRATOR

Matthew Vimislik is an illustrator and game designer working in New York, USA. He lives with his wife, two cats and possibly a family of Black-billed Cuckoo birds that has made a nest in his meticulously preened hair.

OUT OF THIS WORLD

I'm Starr and I'm just like every other ten-year-old girl I know, with one big difference ... I live in space!

You see, my mum is a world-class astronaut, scientist and all round super genius. Now she's not just my mum, she's also in charge of the world's most advanced space station. People can visit here on holiday and it's my job to make sure they have a great time. My best friend, Allison, thinks I'll forget all about her now that I live in space, but just because I live in space doesn't mean I don't need my best friend. I may be a regular girl, but my life is completely out of this world!

READ THEM ALL!

ROLL UP, ROLL UP!

Meet **Lizzie Brown**, the circus's youngest ever fortuneteller, and her friends, the crime-solving **Penny Gaff Gang**!

Lizzie Brown has escaped the slums of Victorian London and joined Fitzy's Travelling Circus. By accident, she discovers that she has an amazing ability: in a world of charlatans and tricksters, Lizzie may be the only truly clairvoyant palm reader in existence! Lizzie musters together her gang of circus children – the Penny Gaff Gang, all with their own amazing talents – to use her visions to solve mysteries.

The
MAGNIFICENT
LIZZIE BROWN
and the
Mysterious
Phantom
VICKI LOCKWOOD
The
MAGNIFICENT
LIZZIE BROWN
and the
Devil's
Hound
VICKI LOCKWOOD
The
MAGNIFICENT
LIZZIE BROWN
and the
Ghost
Ship
VICKI LOCKWOOD
The
MAGNIFICENT
LIZZIE BROWN
and the
Fairy
Child
VICKI LOCKWOOD